HELLO KITTY

and friends

♥ ♥ ♥

The Treasure Hunt

HELLO KITTY
and friends

The Treasure Hunt

HarperCollins *Children's Books*

MEET HELLO KITTY

and friends

Mimmy

Hello Kitty

Tammy

Mama

Papa

Grandpa

Grandma

Fifi

Dear Daniel

First published in Great Britain by HarperCollins *Children's Books* in 2013

www.harpercollins.co.uk
1 3 5 7 9 10 8 6 4 2
ISBN: 978-000-751570-7

Printed and bound in England by Clays Ltd, St Ives plc.

MIX
Paper from
responsible sources
FSC C007454

FSC™ is a non-profit international organisation established to promote
the responsible management of the world's forests. Products carrying the
FSC label are independently certified to assure consumers that they come
from forests that are managed to meet the social, economic and
ecological needs of present and future generations,
and other controlled sources.

Find out more about HarperCollins and the environment at
www.harpercollins.co.uk/green

Contents

A Great Idea

Hello Kitty put the paper into a neat pile

on the shelves of the school art cupboard. She'd

already sorted the paintbrushes into different

pots and sharpened the pencils, and put them

all away.

Her teacher Miss Davey came in, and took a look around. A big **smile** spread over her face as she exclaimed at what a great job Hello Kitty had done! The cupboard had never been so tidy. Miss Davey thanked her for all her hard work, and for volunteering to clear it out. It had taken Hello Kitty most of her lunch break.

Hello Kitty had been very happy to help! She asked if Miss Davey needed her to finish sorting the paints out by colour, but Miss Davey told her that

they could leave that for another day. Hello

Kitty nodded happily and skipped off to find her

friends. She **l♥ved** helping people!

Her friends Tammy and Fifi were sitting at

a table in their empty classroom, heads bent

over pieces of paper. It was strange not seeing

Dear Daniel with them. Dear Daniel was Hello

Kitty's other really good

friend but he was away

travelling with his dad,

and was missing the

first few days of the

school term – he had

gotten permission for it

earlier in the year. Hello Kitty

was organising a **big** welcome home party

for him in three days time. She still needed to

get some decorations and food and sort out

the games, and she made a list in her head as

she went over to where Fifi and Tammy were

sitting. Suddenly, one of her special, super, Hello

Kitty ideas popped into her head. Instead of games, what about having a treasure hunt?

Hello Kitty squealed excitedly, and Fifi and Tammy looked up as she quickly started to

tell them her idea for Dear Daniel's welcome home party.

Fifi smiled distractedly, and rubbed something out on her paper.

Tammy nodded and agreed that it was a *great* idea, but she only looked up for a moment.

Hello Kitty blinked. She had thought her friends would be much more excited! Fifi pushed her paper away, and looked up at Hello Kitty again. She sighed, and explained to Hello Kitty that she was

14

sorry she was so distracted. She was trying
to design an ice-skating costume for her new
routine, as she hadn't been able to find anything
that was just right. She had thought it would be
easy, but designing an outfit was harder than
she thought!

Tammy piped up that
she was trying to make
up a story for the school
magazine. She had the
beginning done, but couldn't

decide what should happen next, and it had to
be handed in on Friday!

But they both thought Hello Kitty's idea of a

welcome home treasure hunt did sound good.

Hello Kitty smiled and thanked them, before

declaring that they didn't need to worry about

that for now – it sounded like they needed her

help!

Fifi and Tammy both brightened up at this.

Hello Kitty was so good at designing clothes,

so Fifi knew she'd be a great help with her

costume! And Tammy was just as excited

that she would be able to tell her what she'd

written in her story so far, and have her help

come up with what would happen next. Hello

Kitty **grinned**. There was nothing she liked

better than helping her friends!

2

Being a Good Friend

Hello Kitty sat down next to Fifi, and

questioned her about what sort of ice-skating

costume she wanted. Fifi thought hard about

it. Her routine was about fire – she started off

as a spark, before turning into a big flame, and

at the end she would shrink down into just a
burning ember. It would have lots of **spins**,
so she wanted something really impressive. She
had drawn a red leotard so far.

Hello Kitty could already picture the perfect

dress, and she started to count

ideas out loud on her fingers.

One: Instead of just red, Fifi

could have layers of

orange and yellow too. Two: She

could have a *swirly* skirt,

so when she twirled it would

look like flames. And three: She

could have gold sequins too, to look like sparks

from the fire! Fifi nodded and

clapped her hands excitedly.

Just then the bell went for

afternoon class.

Fifi let out a disappointed sigh. They had only just got started! But Hello Kitty suggested that they have a Friendship Club meeting that afternoon at her house. They could finish drawing her costume then.

Hello Kitty, Fifi, Tammy and Dear Daniel had formed The Friendship Club. They had

The Friendship Club

meetings at each other's houses where they made things and played and thought up rules about friendship. Hello Kitty was just telling Fifi that she would ask her Mama if it was OK for them to have a meeting, when she remembered something. **Oh no!** She had promised Mama she would help her make jewellery that night. Mama loved to make jewellery and Hello Kitty liked to help out when she could. So she wouldn't be able to meet that evening.

Fifi had an ice-skating lesson after school the next day, but she suggested that Tammy and Hello Kitty could both come along, and they could have the Friendship Club meeting at the ice rink café afterwards!

Tammy agreed enthusiastically. She **l♥ved** the hot chocolate there! And Hello Kitty put in that while Fifi was skating, Hello Kitty would be able to help Tammy with her story too. It was perfect!

Tammy beamed, and thanked her. But she was wondering if Hello Kitty needed help with anything too; the treasure hunt sounded like a **lot** of work. Could they help her with it, she asked?

Hello Kitty reassured her that she was fine, and everything was under control. They

just needed to be at the park at ten-thirty on
Saturday morning, ready to have some fun! Fifi
spun round, her hair flying out. A Hello Kitty
party – she couldn't wait! *Hooray!*

In the car on the way home, Hello Kitty
told her twin sister Mimmy, and Mama and
Papa, about her plans for the treasure hunt.
She invited them to come along on Saturday
morning. Mimmy might not be able to as her
flute exam was on then, but the exam was on
early so they should be back in time! Mimmy
smiled a bit nervously. She was a bit worried

about her exam, she explained, so at least the treasure hunt afterwards was something to look forward to.

Hello Kitty was surprised that Mimmy was worried. She was **great** at the flute. But Mimmy just didn't feel like she'd practised enough. She gave out a loud sigh, so Mama reminded her that she still had three more days

until her exam! She could practise every evening

until then.

Hello Kitty offered to listen to Mimmy play.

She knew Mimmy would feel more confident if

she listened and could tell her how **good**

she was. Mimmy brightened up

and thanked her. That

would really help. And

Hello Kitty would

help Mama with

her jewellery that

evening as well. She

knew that Mama

needed to make more than usual this time, as some very good friends of hers were having a party that Friday and she wanted to take some along as presents for them.

With the jewellery and Mimmy's exam and Dear Daniel's treasure hunt, it was going to be a *busy few days*. But Hello Kitty smiled. She liked being busy!

After they got home, Hello Kitty sat down with Mama and helped make jewellery. It was lovely, sitting and chatting together. Hello

Kitty threaded beads on to
cords for Mama, who added
knots and clasps to make bracelets
and necklaces. At six o'clock, they
stopped working when Papa
came home.

As they stood up, Mama told her what
a big help she'd been, and Hello Kitty offered to
help again tomorrow. Mama smiled and nodded
as she walked to the kitchen. It was time for her
and Papa to make supper.

After a yummy
supper followed by
bananas and ice cream,

Hello Kitty went upstairs and listened to Mimmy playing the flute. She had meant to use the evening to write the invitations to the treasure hunt but as Mimmy finished, Mama said it was time for bed. **Oh well!** She'd just have to do them before school, thought Hello Kitty as she brushed her teeth.

Mimmy *yawned* as she went past the
bathroom door, and thanked her for listening.
She asked nervously if Hello Kitty could listen
to her tomorrow too. Hello Kitty promised
she would.

Mimmy said good night and Hello Kitty went

to her bedroom and climbed into bed. Pulling

her duvet up around her, she

thought about everything

she had to do – listen to

Mimmy, make

jewellery with Mama, help

Tammy with her story and

Fifi with her dress, as well as

organising Dear Daniel's treasure hunt. Could

she do it all?

Of course she could, she thought, and

snuggled down to sleep.

3

So Much to Do

When Hello Kitty woke up, sunlight was

shining through her curtains. She looked at her

alarm clock. It was really early. **Great!** If

she got up now she would have plenty of time

to get things done before school. She went

to her desk and made a list of everything she

needed to do for Dear Daniel's treasure hunt:

1. Write invitations and email
   Dear Daniel!
2. Make decorations and banner
3. Make the treasure chest!
4. Work out clues
5. Pack up everything for
   the picnic
6. SET THE TREASURE HUNT UP!

Next, she tiptoed downstairs and wrote

the invitations out on pieces of white card,

decorating each with a picture of a treasure

chest spilling over with treasure. Finally she went on the computer in the study. The twins were allowed to use it to email their friends. She emailed Dear Daniel, to tell him that they were missing him, as well as all about Fifi's ice-skating costume and Tammy's story. Lastly, she made sure he would be free on Saturday at ten-thirty, because she had a surprise for him! She would meet him in the park. She signed off Lots of Love, *Hello Kitty xx*

Just then she heard a noise behind her. Mama was standing in the doorway in her dressing gown, yawning. Hello Kitty explained that she had gotten up early as she had so much to do! She hadn't had time to email Dear Daniel and get the invitations done the night before.

Mama came over and kissed the top of her head. It had been because Hello Kitty had been too busy helping Mama and Mimmy

that she hadn't had time to do her own things!

Mama asked Hello Kitty if she was sure she

wasn't trying to do too much.

Hello Kitty shook her head. Definitely not,

she asserted — it was **fun!** Mama smiled and

said as long as she was happy then; that was

the most important thing. But it was time to get

ready for school now. Hello Kitty jumped up to

get dressed. She didn't want to be late!

As soon as Hello Kitty hurried into the

playground that morning, Fifi asked if she was

able to come to the ice rink that evening. Hello

Kitty smiled and nodded. Tammy was anxious

to work on her story too, but she relaxed now

that she knew Hello Kitty would be helping her

later on.

Hello Kitty smiled as she promised she would help them both, and then fished into her bag and handed them each an invitation.

Fifi read hers straightaway. She couldn't **wait!** And Tammy was excited too. In her head, Hello Kitty ticked off the first thing to do on her list. But there was still lots to do – she'd have to get going on the rest tonight!

After school, Fifi's mum took them to the ice rink. Hello Kitty and Tammy skated for a while and then watched Fifi with her ice-skating teacher. As Fifi spun and leapt, Hello Kitty sketched an outfit in her notebook. She drew a dress which had a skirt made from layers of yellow, orange and red fabric. Then she coloured the top in red and added lots of sparkling sequins scattered all over. There – *perfect!*

Fifi finished her training session and came off the ice. She took off her skates, and they all

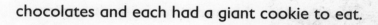

went to the café. They had

half an hour before

Fifi's mum collected

them. They ordered hot

chocolates and each had a giant cookie to eat.

Fifi asked eagerly if Hello Kitty had had any

costume ideas while she had been skating. Hello

Kitty showed her the

drawing. Fifi studied

it, and her face lit up.

She **l♥ved** it!

She would show it to

her mum, and they

could have it made.

She gave Hello Kitty a big hug and thanked her.

Tammy suggested Fifi should wear something in

her hair too. Oohhh! Hello Kitty had a red and

gold bow that would look great, and

Fifi could wear golden glitter

on her cheeks too. She told

Fifi she could bring them in

tomorrow. She would look

totally *SUPER!*

Fifi grinned and blushed happily.

They talked about the outfit so much that

Hello Kitty didn't have time to read Tammy's

story. But she suggested that if she called Mama

to ask, she could come back to Tammy's house

now and they could go through it. Tammy

thought that would be great! It was fine with

Mama, so Fifi's mum dropped them both at

Tammy's house. After waving goodbye, they

ran upstairs to Tammy's

bedroom. Hello

Kitty liked Tammy's

room. It had books

everywhere!

Tammy sat down on her bed to explain her story. So far, it was about four friends who found a **magic** carpet one day. The carpet could take them anywhere! She'd written the start, but was having trouble coming up with adventures for them to have.

Hello Kitty was full of ideas! What about going to the zoo? Maybe the magic of the carpet could make the animals talk. Or they could go to a tropical island and find treasure... She chattered on.

Tammy liked both of those ideas, and now that they were both thinking together she was finding it easier to come up with her own. The two of them talked and talked.

By the time Papa arrived to pick her up, Hello Kitty felt tired out. She'd been so *busy* imagining all sorts of adventures that it almost felt as though she had lived them all!

Tammy was delighted. She would finish the story that night, but she wanted Hello Kitty to help her decorate it too, so it would look great when she handed it in.

Hello Kitty said she'd be happy to! She could bring her **sparkly** pens to use too. Tammy told her what a good friend she was, and Hello Kitty smiled and hugged her goodbye. She got into the car with Papa and yawned. It seemed like a long time since she had got up that morning. It had been very busy day!

Papa saw her yawn and suggested that since she'd had such an early start, she should have a nice early night too. The thought of going to bed was **very** tempting but Hello Kitty shook her head. It was only two days until Dear Daniel's treasure hunt. She still had so much to do! And of course she'd promised Mimmy and Mama she would help them as well. She told Papa not to worry.

When they got home, Mimmy came charging down the stairs with her flute, ready for Hello Kitty to listen to her play. Hello Kitty nodded and smiled, and started to follow her up the stairs. But just then, Mama called out and came into the hall. She needed help with finishing the bracelets that she was working on. Was Hello Kitty still able to help?

So Hello Kitty and Mimmy both went and helped with the bracelets and then Hello Kitty listened to Mimmy practise for her exam. By the time she fell into bed that night she was very tired and still hadn't got any further with the treasure hunt preparations!

She **promised** herself she would finish them tomorrow as she set her alarm to wake up very early. Then she put her head on her pillow and fell fast asleep.

4

Busy, Busy, Busy!

Hello Kitty woke to the ringing of her

alarm clock. She turned it off and yawned.

She felt like staying in her warm bed but she had

too much to do! She put on her fluffy pink

dressing gown and went to check the computer.

There was an email from Dear Daniel waiting

for her!

HK mail new reply delete

inbox
junk
sent

Dear Hello Kitty,
I'm having a great time. There are so many animals here! I can come to the park on Saturday; we get back on Friday night. What are you planning?
Love, Dear Daniel x

Kitty smiled to herself and wrote him a quick reply:

HK mail new reply delete

inbox
junk
sent

Hello Dear Daniel!
That's super about Saturday, but I can't tell you what I'm planning – it's a SURPRISE! Have lots of fun today. I'd better go and get ready for school now!
Love Hello Kitty xx

She clicked 'send'. Now she should

get on with the decorations!

She went to the cupboard in the

kitchen and took out some strings

of paper flags. She would ask Mama to buy

some balloons, and she would make a banner

saying,

WELCOME HOME, DEAR DANIEL!

In the scrap material box she found an old

white sheet that Mama had said she could have.

She had just started cutting it up when Mama

came in, commenting that Hello Kitty was up

early again! Hello Kitty looked up and smiled.

She had lots to do! Speaking to Mama reminded her that she had to take some things into school for Tammy and Fifi. She **jumped** up to fetch her sparkly pens and the glitter and bow. On her way up the stairs she bumped into Mimmy, who looked flustered. She'd been trying to work out what to wear to her music exam the next

day, and she couldn't decide! She knew Hello

Kitty was great at choosing clothes, so would

she be able to come and help her, she asked?

Hello Kitty nodded and smiled. **Phew!**

Mimmy breathed a sigh of relief.

They ran upstairs to choose an outfit. They

picked out a smart black skirt that Hello Kitty

matched with a white blouse

with puff sleeves from

her own wardrobe.

That was one of the

best things about

being twins – they

could always share

clothes! Mimmy tried them on with some ballet pumps. It was *perfect!* She grinned as she looked in the mirror, and hugged Hello Kitty just as Mama called up to them. They needed to get ready for school, or they'd be late! Hello Kitty dashed into her room and started pulling on her school uniform. She only had time to give her hair a quick brush and grab a quick breakfast, before she jumped into the car with Mimmy and Papa.

When Hello Kitty got to school, she saw Tammy sitting on a bench reading. She ran

over, and the first thing Tammy asked was if

Hello Kitty had remembered the glitter pens.

She had finished her story and printed it out so

they could start decorating it!

Oh no! Hello Kitty clapped her hand to

her mouth. She had been distracted with Mimmy

on her way to get her pens. She said sorry

and as she spoke, she realised she hadn't

brought the glitter and bow for

Fifi either! She had left

them at home too.

Tammy comforted her with a hug. She could

use her own pens to decorate the story, and

Fifi didn't need her things that day anyway! It

wasn't a big deal at all. Hello Kitty offered to

bring her *glitter* pens to the treasure hunt

the next day, so they could work on it then.

She really did want to help.

But Tammy needed to hand

the story in today. It was OK

though, as she had her own pens, and could **maybe** even use some glitter from the art cupboard! She hugged Hello Kitty again, and reminded her how much she had on, with helping everyone and organising the party. What if she and Fifi helped with the treasure

hunt, she suggested.
They could come
round after school
and do it together –
as a **Friendship
Club** thing!

Hello Kitty shook her head quickly. She
wanted Tammy and Fifi to be able to enjoy the
treasure hunt too, and they wouldn't be able
to if they already knew the clues! She almost
had everything ready, she assured Tammy. She
crossed her fingers. She wanted her friends to
really enjoy themselves!

Tammy asked if she was sure.

Hello Kitty smiled at her and nodded. She took a deep breath as she realised the party was the very next day. But everything would be ready by then. Of course it would!

Disaster!

As soon as Hello Kitty got home from school,

she went to her bedroom and started finishing

the banner for the party. She had to get it done

quickly so she could start baking the biscuits

and cakes. And she still needed to work out the

treasure hunt clues and get the things for the

picnic together! But even though she wanted

to be fast, it took **ages** to paint the banner

and add in sparkles and stars. She was still

painting after tea.

Mimmy came in to see how it was going just

as Hello Kitty finally finished. Hello Kitty told

her things were coming along, but she still had

lots to do! Mimmy looked surprised. She had

been going to do a final practice

for her music exam, but offered

to help get things ready for

the party instead. Hello

Kitty shook her head – she

didn't want Mimmy not practising because of her! But just then, she looked at the banner and decorations and realised she didn't have any balloons. **Oh no!** It was too late to buy them now.

Mimmy went off to practice, and told Hello Kitty to call her if she needed a hand. Hello Kitty nodded and went down to the kitchen. She wished Mama was around to help, but Mama was at her friends' party for the evening. Hello Kitty rushed

around, throwing ingredients into a bowl and

whisking madly as she thought about the things

she still had to do. Then she spooned the cake

mixture into cases. Hmmm, it didn't look

as smooth as it normally did.

Oh well!

Papa came into

the kitchen to turn

on the oven. He

commented that it

was a bit late for

baking, but Hello

Kitty explained she needed to get the cakes ready for the party the next day. Papa helped her open the oven and put the cakes inside, and Hello Kitty *yawned.* Papa glanced at her. She was looking very tired, he said, and bedtime was in half an hour! Just enough time to take the cakes out of the oven and get ready for bed.

Hello Kitty swallowed. Half an hour wasn't nearly enough time to get everything done!

She'd just have to get up early in the morning
again, she decided. She hurried about, packing
plates, cups and a tablecloth into a bag for the
picnic and checking she had all the decorations.
Suddenly, she smelt burning. Oh no! **The
cakes!**

She called out to Papa.

He appeared in the kitchen, and carefully they
opened the oven door. The cakes were all burnt
on top. Oh dear! Papa looked at Hello Kitty.
They could make some more
tomorrow, he reassured
her. But now, it was
time for bed. Hello Kitty

nodded and they headed upstairs. After she
cleaned her teeth and got into bed, Papa kissed
her goodnight and turned off the light.

Hello Kitty lay in bed, her thoughts racing.
She was tired but she didn't feel sleepy. All she
could think about was the next day. Maybe
she could do the treasure hunt clues
now? That would leave her
enough time to make
cakes in the morning.
She reached for
the torch on her
bedside table.
Turning it on, she

tiptoed across her bedroom and fetched some paper and a pen, and got back into bed.

Where could she hide the clues in the park and where would the treasure be? Maybe the first clue could lead to the the swings. She wrote down:

Go to the place where people swing high –
Search down on the ground, not up in the sky!

Now, what about the second clue? She shut her eyes and thought about the park. Maybe it should be by the climbing frame, or the bench or even by the pond…

Knock, knock! Hello Kitty woke with a start. Her torch was lying beside her and the paper and pens had rolled on to the floor in the night. Papa came into the room, smiling. She sleepily asked what time it was, and glanced at the clock.

72

Nine o'clock! Hello Kitty *squeaked* and sat up in bed. She must have been tired. Mimmy had already gone to her exam, and she hadn't even woken up. Papa reminded her that she had wanted to get to the park by nine-thirty to set everything up, so they would have to leave soon.

Oh no! She didn't have everything ready. Papa asked her what was wrong, and Hello Kitty looked at him in dismay. She still didn't have food for the party or clues for the treasure hunt.

Whatever was she going to do?

The Treasure Hunt

Papa hugged Hello Kitty as she blurted out

what had happened. Dear Daniel's party was

going to be a disaster!

Papa sat back and looked at her. He told

her everything would be fine, but she had

been trying to do too much on her own! He reminded her that she could always ask for help if she needed it. After all, that's what friends and family were for!

Hello Kitty nodded. She knew he was right, but she had wanted to do everything herself so everyone else would be able to have fun following the clues and doing the treasure hunt! Papa winked at her, and stood up to take her downstairs. What was going on? But then she smelled something **l♥vely**...

Hello Kitty ran downstairs and saw three plates of freshly baked cakes and biscuits. She gasped.

Papa explained that Mama and Mimmy had

seen the burnt cakes that morning, before

Mimmy's exam. So they had decided it was

time Hello Kitty had some help! Papa's eyes

twinkled as he suggested she give Fifi and

Tammy a call, and he would start packing the

car for the picnic. Maybe if everyone worked together, they would get the Treasure Hunt ready on time after all!

Hello Kitty phoned Tammy first. As soon as Hello Kitty asked for help, Tammy squealed with excitement. She'd been wishing she could help the whole time! She had **loads** of balloons and streamers, and she would bring them to the park. She would see Hello Kitty soon she declared, and hung up the phone.

Fifi was just as keen to help. She could bring
crisps and drinks and she even had a treasure
chest for the end of the hunt!

Hello Kitty **gasped**. The treasure! She
didn't have any!

Fifi giggled and told
her not to worry.
She would stop at
the shops on the
way to the park,
and she and her mum
would pick up some
sweets. She hung up.

Hello Kitty breathed deeply. Maybe

everything was going to be all right after all!

She thought of Tammy and Fifi and smiled.

Thank goodness for friends!

They all met at the park. They lay out the

picnic blankets and while Tammy and Fifi put

out the food and Hello Kitty invented and hid

the clues, Papa hung the flags and the banner

from the trees. At ten o'clock, Mama and

Mimmy turned up too. Hello Kitty hugged them

both, and thanked them for doing all the baking

that morning. Whatever would she have done

without them! Mama smiled and told her it

was the least they could do after all she'd been

doing for them the last few days!

Hello Kitty turned to Mimmy, and asked how

her exam had gone. But she already knew, as

Mimmy's cheeks were pink with happiness!
Mimmy confirmed that she'd passed. It had
gone really well. Mama agreed, but for now,
both of them wanted to know what they could
do to help.

Hello Kitty looked to see
what still needed doing. There
were the **balloons** to blow
up, the treasure chest to fill... she
listed all the tasks.

Mama went to get started, but first
she gave Hello Kitty a little bag. She'd also
brought her something to add

to the treasure chest!
Hello Kitty peeped
inside. There were five
friendship bracelets
there – each had a little
silver disc with their

initials engraved on them.
The girls' bracelets were
in bright colours and
Dear Daniel's was black
and green. Hello Kitty
jumped for **joy!**
They were brilliant and
she grabbed Mama in a big
hug. She'd better go and hide them
in the treasure chest straightaway!

By ten-thirty, everything was ready. The
food was all beautifully arranged on plates,

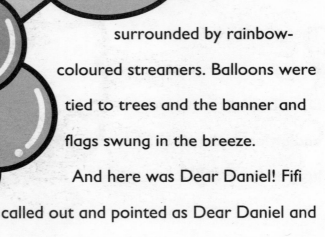

surrounded by rainbow-coloured streamers. Balloons were tied to trees and the banner and flags swung in the breeze.

And here was Dear Daniel! Fifi called out and pointed as Dear Daniel and his dad came through the park gates.

Dear Daniel saw them and broke into a *run*. Hello Kitty, Fifi and Tammy raced to meet him. Hello Kitty reached

him first and gave him a big hug. Fifi and Tammy hugged him too. They'd missed him!

Dear Daniel had missed them all too. He had a big smile as he told them he'd had a great time, but it was brilliant to be back. He looked around at all the party stuff in delight. **Wow!** It all looked super, and he was very impressed.

And it wasn't just the food,
put in Tammy. Hello
Kitty had organised
a treasure hunt too.
Hello Kitty blushed
happily, and suggested they
all have a cake. Then they could
get started! Mimmy was pouring out drinks
for everyone. They tucked into the cakes and
biscuits while the grown-ups had coffee and tea
and chatted about Dear Daniel's trip.

The cakes were
really yummy! Dear
Daniel munched on

a chocolate one. He always thought Hello Kitty made the best cakes. But Hello Kitty explained that Mimmy and Mama had made them. And Fifi and Tammy helped with all the decorations. She **smiled** at her friends. They had all worked together to get the party ready! Happiness filled her. She'd wanted to organise the party on her own but actually it had been even more fun with everyone helping.

Mimmy pointed out that Hello Kitty did do the treasure hunt on her own though. And it was time for the first clue! Hello Kitty handed out a piece of card which had the rhyme about the swings on it. It would lead them to another

clue, which would lead to another clue... There were ten clues altogether and at the end of it was the treasure!

Dear Daniel jumped to his feet and grinned at the others. What were they waiting for? It was time to get *started!*

The treasure hunt was a huge success. Dear Daniel and the others **l♥ved** following the clues and at last they found the treasure chest hidden deep inside the hollow of a bush. They opened it up and cheered as they emptied out the sweets and bracelets.

Fifi announced that it was the best treasure hunt ever.

And Dear Daniel declared that it was the **best** welcome home party ever too! Hello Kitty admitted that they nearly hadn't had a party at all. It had only turned out so well because everyone had helped out.

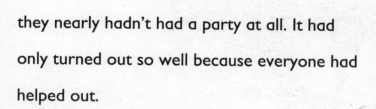

Tammy linked arms with her. That was what friends were for, she said.

Mimmy nodded. Friends never minded helping

out, she explained. And Hello Kitty should remember that, and ask them for help next time she needed it! Hello Kitty nodded. She definitely would!

Fifi turned a cartwheel, and bounced up with a gasp. She had an idea! They should have a new Friendship Club rule!

Good friends are always there to share the load.

It was *brilliant!* They all agreed to add it to their list.

Dear Daniel looked over towards the food on the blankets, and suggested another rule. What about: Good friends should always be there to help you eat cakes! They all laughed.

Giggling together, they hurried across the grass towards the picnic. Hello Kitty linked arms with Tammy, feeling so **happy** she could burst. She was with her three friends having fun — what could be better than that?

The end

Turn over the page for activities and
fun things that you can do with your
friends – just like Hello Kitty!

It's Treasure Hunt Time!

Everybody loves to play hide and seek, but it can be even more fun if you and your friends aren't looking for each other... You're looking for treasure instead!

Follow the instructions on the following pages to set up a fun trail of clues for your friends to follow, and some great ideas for a treasure at the end!

Where do I start?

You will need four things to start your treasure hunt.

1. People to play – why not ask your family, or friends? It could even be part of a party...

2. A safe area to set out your treasure hunt. This can be inside if you don't have outside space; in your back garden, or even in an area of the park. Don't forget to take a grown-up with you if you go to the park!

3. Clues! These will lead people to your treasure. Try to have at least four before you get to the treasure – but not too many or people might get lost! Check out pages 100 and 101 for some head-scratching clue ideas to try.

4. And finally – the Treasure! See page 102 for some super ideas.

Let's Get Hunting...

You need to start at the finish for a treasure hunt!

Figure out where you want to hide your treasure, and works backwards from there. When you have decided, you need to go back along the path you want your hunters to take, and decide on each place a clue will be hidden – all the way back to the start! Try to move around to keep it exciting.

Get a clue!

Now you have figured out where to hide them, you can write your clues! Each clue should lead the player to the next one, until the last one leads them on to the treasure... check out the ideas on the next page to keep your hunters guessing.

- **Poetry clues!** Look in the place where you keep your clothes. Is it in a pocket? Nobody knows! (Answer: in the wardrobe).
- **Question Clues!** Where do you find knives, forks, and spoons? (Answer: in the kitchen drawer).
- **Drawing Clues!** A drawing of the big tree in the backyard, with an X marking where the next clue is.
- **Map clues!** A map of the park, with a dotted line to show where to go and an X marking the spot!
- **Coded clues!** You can use a simple number code to hide the answer to where the treasure is.

A	B	C	D	E	F	G	H	I	J	K	L	M	N	O	P	Q	R	S	T	U	V	W	X	Y	Z
1	2	3	4	5	6	7	8	9	10	11	12	13	14	15	16	17	18	19	20	21	22	23	24	25	26

N E X T _ T O _ T H E _ S W I N G S !
14 5 24 20   20 15   20 8 5   19 23 9 14 7 19

(Answer: Next to the swings!)

The Treasure!

Hooray – your hunters have finally reached the end of your treasure hunt! But what will they find? Your treasure should be small enough to hide, but still something nice. Try some of these ideas:

- Sweets
- Photos of you together
- Small toys
- Friendship Bracelets (see page 104 for how to make these!)

And what about the treasure chest?

You can decorate it with pictures, patterns, sequins or anything you like – Hello Kitty always makes hers sparkly!

Make your own friendship bracelet

These are great fun to make, and a wonderful treasure for your friends to find!

MAKE SURE YOU ASK MAMA OR PAPA TO HELP!

You will need:

- 3 different coloured strands of thread
- Scissors
- Tape

1. Ask your grown-up helper to cut three pieces of thread in different colours; each about 60cm long – or about the length of your arm.
2. Tie your threads together at one end with one knot. If it's hard, ask a grown-up to help you!
3. Tape the knot to a flat surface like a table, and lay the three strands separate from each other.

MAKE SURE YOU ASK MAMA OR PAPA TO HELP!

4. Plait them all together, just like you would your hair! By putting one over the other so that they all weave together.
5. When you get to the end, tie the ends together into a knot (or ask your grown-up helper to), and snip off any straggly ends.
6. Wow! You've made a beautiful friendship bracelet!

Turn the page for a sneak peek at

HELLO KITTY

and friends'

next adventure...

The Talent Show

BBrrrring! Hello Kitty rang the doorbell.
She waited excitedly as she heard the sound
of running footsteps and then the door was
thrown open. Her friends Fifi, Tammy and Dear
Daniel stood inside. They were all members
of the Friendship Club, which they had started
together after they all met at school. They held
fun meetings, went on trips out together and

made up rules about friendship.

That Saturday they were having a special Friendship Club meeting at Fifi's – they had decided to hold a toy fashion show! Hello Kitty had her fluffy white bear with her. She could see that all her friends had toys too – Fifi had a tiger, Tammy had a rabbit and Dear Daniel had a zebra. Hello Kitty couldn't wait to get started!

They all said hello and hurried upstairs. Fifi had made a catwalk for the toys in her bedroom. She had made it out of shoeboxes glued together with material stuck on top. It looked really super! All the toys had come from a special shop where you could buy different clothes to dress your toy in. The four friends put the outfits they had brought on to Fifi's bed and then they each selected something for their toy to wear. Dear Daniel wanted Stripy his zebra to wear sporty clothes. But would it be a football kit or a karate kit or a skateboard kit? He decided on the football kit.

Tammy put Floppy, her toy rabbit, into a denim skirt and white T-shirt while Fifi dressed Tasha the tiger in a purple sparkly ice-skating outfit with matching ice skates. Hello Kitty took much longer to decide on what her toy bear, Snowflake, would be wearing. It was so much fun trying out different tops with different skirts, adding scarves and belts and hairbands until the outfit looked perfect. Almost like being a real fashion designer!

While they were waiting for Hello Kitty, Tammy picked up Floppy and Stripy and started pretending to make them talk in silly voices. She made Stripy ask Floppy for a dance and then made Floppy act as if she was really shy! Fifi, Hello Kitty and Dear Daniel giggled loudly. So Tammy put on the same voice as their class teacher Miss Davey had, when she got cross and told them to settle down. She sounded so much like Miss Davey that they all giggled even more.

But now Hello Kitty was finally ready!
Snowflake was wearing a short ruffled red skirt
with a white T-shirt and a red and black striped
waistcoat. She had a matching red and black
hairband, with a sparkly bow and a little red
handbag. She looked super-stylish!

Tammy remarked how nice Snowflake
looked. She wished Floppy looked as good but
she could never work out what clothes went
together. Hello Kitty smiled and offered to help
her. She loved helping her friends! She swapped
Floppy's plain white T-shirt for a strappy pale
blue top with a heart on it and then chose a
navy and pink scarf that she twisted around

Floppy's neck. She added a navy belt and shoes and then finished the look off with a blue hair bow.

She nodded at Tammy and wondered what she thought now...

Find out what happens next in...

Out now!

· A HELLO KITTY STORY ·

HELLO KITTY

and friends

The Talent Show

Coming soon:

A HELLO KITTY CHRISTMAS SPECIAL

TWO SPECIAL CHRISTMAS STORIES

HELLO KITTY
and friends

The Christmas Present

The Friendship Club

The School Trip

The Summer Fair

The Pop Princess

The Wedding Day

The Beach Holiday

The Treasure Hunt

The Talent Show

Collect all of the Hello Kitty and Friends Stories!